BRAIN MATTER

CONTENTS

What Is the Brain? — 2

How Different Parts of the Brain Work — 4

How the Sleeping Brain Works — 8

Memories — 12

How the Brain Controls Body Temperature — 16

Animal Brains — 18

How Brains and Computers Compare — 22

Index — 26

BY JILL EGGLETON

Rigby

BRAIN MATTER

WHAT IS THE BRAIN?

PREDICT:

What information do you think you might find in this chapter?

● ● ▶

The brain is the control room that directs our thinking, feeling, talking, and moving. It operates 24 hours a day. It is the most important organ in our body.

Without a brain we couldn't taste, smell, hear, keep our balance, feel happy, feel scared, remember, or dream.

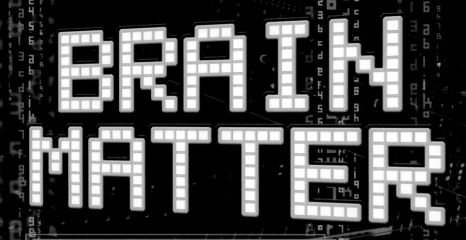

▶ Illustrative diagram of the brain

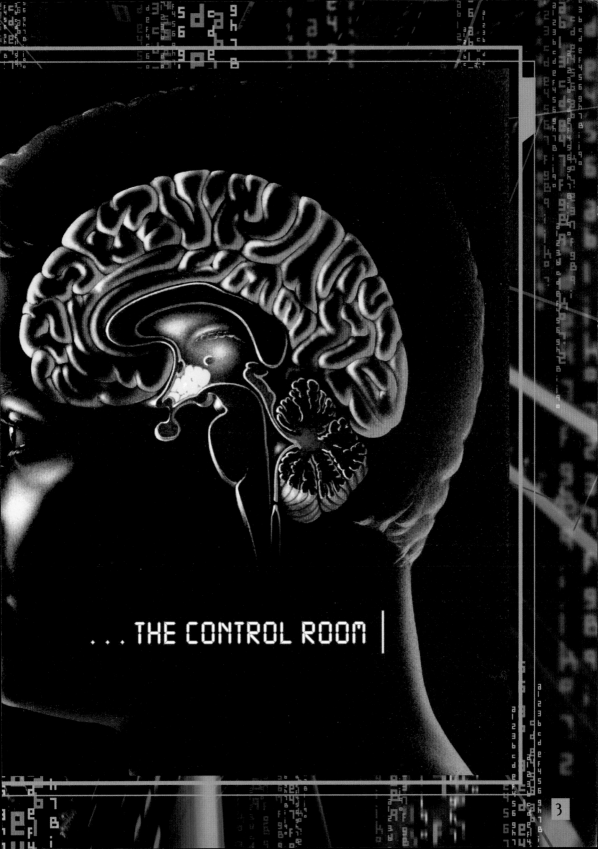

. . . THE CONTROL ROOM |

HOW DIFFERENT PARTS OF THE BRAIN WORK

Different parts of our brains control all the different things that happen in our bodies. The top part of the brain is divided into two domes. It looks like a wrinkly walnut. The cortex (the outer layer of the brain) is used to receive and interpret incoming sensory information. We use it to control movement and think and feel. It is the part that makes us aware of what we are doing.

Each side of our brain works with the opposite side of our body. Each side is also in charge of different kinds of thoughts and actions. The left side controls, for example, speech/language, doing things in order (such as tying shoe laces, mathematics . . .)

The right side controls the way we think in pictures. If you were drawing a map of how to get to school, you would use this part of the brain to picture the route in your head.

► Illustrative diagram showing areas of thought

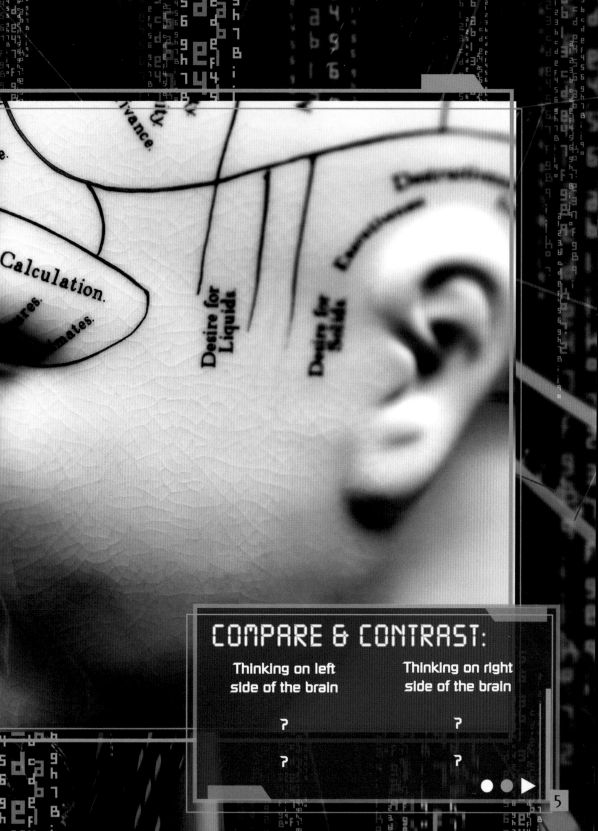

Calculation.

Desire for Liquids

Desire for Solids

COMPARE & CONTRAST:

Thinking on left side of the brain	Thinking on right side of the brain
?	?
?	?

5

Inside the brain are billions of tiny nerve cells called neurons. A neuron looks like a tiny octopus, but with many more tentacles.

In all the different parts of our brain, neurons are sending and receiving signals that allow us to move, hear, taste, see, smell, remember, feel, and think.

Some neurons send and receive messages about what is happening inside and outside the body. The brain decides what should be done.

If your brain receives a message about how good a hamburger smells, for example, it might send a message to your arm to reach out and grab it.

▶ Enlarged view of neuron (nerve cell)

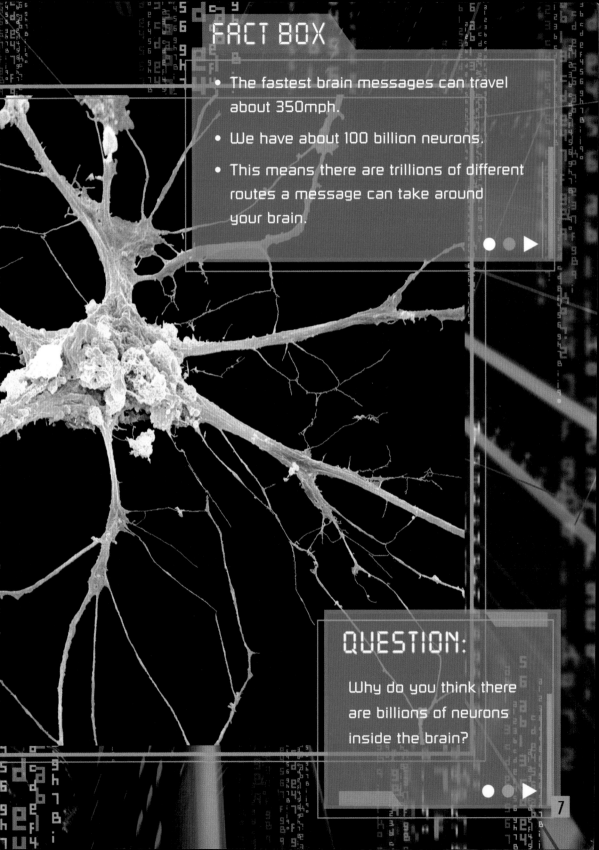

FACT BOX

- The fastest brain messages can travel about 350mph.

- We have about 100 billion neurons.

- This means there are trillions of different routes a message can take around your brain.

QUESTION:

Why do you think there are billions of neurons inside the brain?

HOW THE SLEEPING BRAIN WORKS

Most people spend about one third of their lives asleep. Even when we are asleep, our brain is at work.

Scientists have studied sleep to try and find out what the brain and the body do at this time.

SLEEPING STAGES

When we fall asleep, we go through different stages.

STAGE 1:

* a floating feeling
* breathing slows down
* heartbeat slows down
* muscles relax
* any slight noise will wake you up

STAGE 2:

* eyes roll slowly beneath closed eyelids
* louder noises are needed to wake you up

▶ A sleep laboratory

HEARTBEAT SLOWS DOWN |

PREDICT:
What do you think the rest of the sleep stages might be like?

● ● ▶

STAGE 3:

* heartbeat, breathing, and blood pressure fall
* body temperature falls
* muscles are more relaxed

STAGE 4:

You are now deeply asleep. You might talk in your sleep or even sleep walk. Over the next 30 to 40 minutes this pattern is reversed and the brain and body head back toward Stage One.

Back at Stage One, your eyes start to flicker and your heartbeat becomes irregular. This is known as REM (Rapid Eye Movement sleep). If you are woken up at this time you might say you were in the middle of a dream.

Some scientists think that when we are asleep, the brain sorts information it has received during the day. Some information it gets rid of and some it files in our memories.

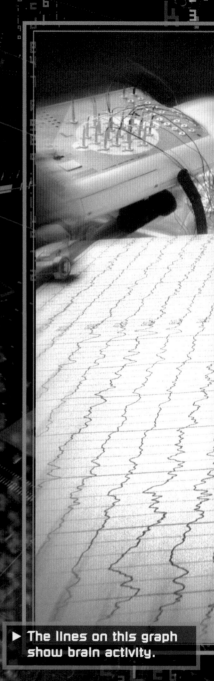

► The lines on this graph show brain activity.

QUESTION:

What information do you think the brain might get rid of?

MEMORIES

Everything we learn and all our experiences are encoded in our brains. This is our memory. Everybody has two types of memory.

LONG-TERM MEMORY:

Our long-term memory stores everything we know.

By the time we are about eight years old, our long-term memory holds more information than a million encyclopedias. It may hold:

- a vocabulary of more than 15,000 words
- the names of all your classmates at school
- how to find your way home
- what you did on your vacation

Things can stay in our long-term memories for hours, weeks, months, years, or our whole lives.

Our long-term memory will never become full. It can go on storing new information even if we live until we are over 100 years old.

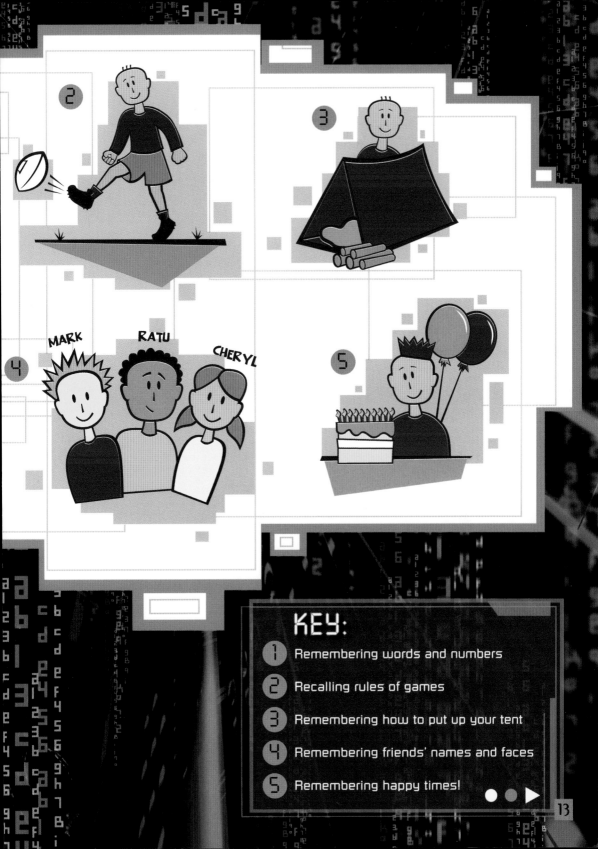

KEY:
1. Remembering words and numbers
2. Recalling rules of games
3. Remembering how to put up your tent
4. Remembering friends' names and faces
5. Remembering happy times!

SHORT-TERM MEMORY:

Our untrained short-term memories can only store about nine things at one time. Most people cannot manage more than seven.

Nothing stays in our short-term memories for more than a few minutes.

After a few minutes, facts in our short-term memories are replaced by new ones. They just fade away or they are transferred to our long-term memory.

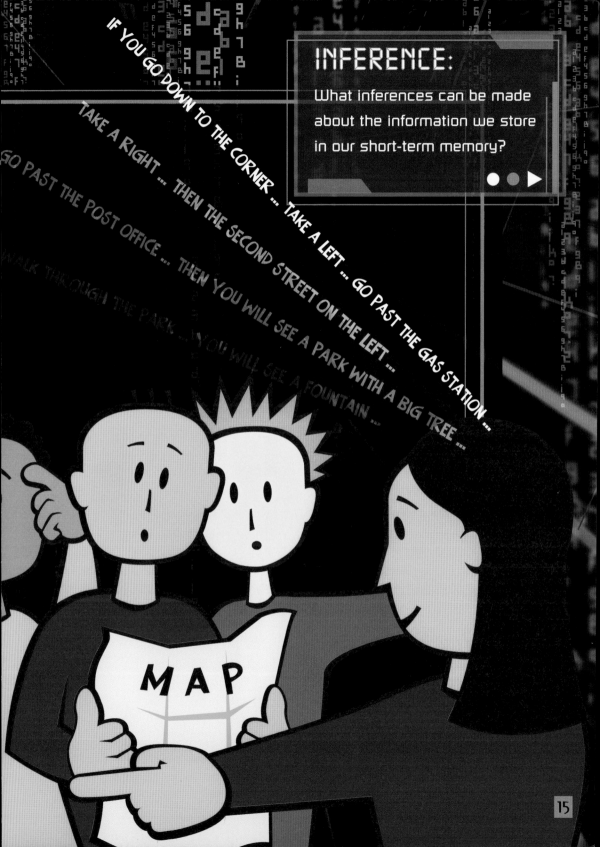

HOW THE BRAIN CONTROLS BODY TEMPERATURE

▶ The hypothalamus

If we are in a hot place or a cold place or somewhere in between, our brain tries to keep the conditions inside our bodies the same.

The hypothalamus is the part of the brain that controls our body temperature.

IF WE ARE GETTING TOO HOT:

- We perspire to cool down the body.
- Hairs lie flat so warm air can be kept away from the skin.
- Our blood flows nearer to the surface of the skin.
- Our muscles relax because movement produces heat.

IF WE ARE GETTING TOO COLD:

- We shiver — jerky movements produce heat.
- Our blood flows away from the skin.
- Hairs on our body stand up so they can trap warm air next to the skin.

TOO HOT

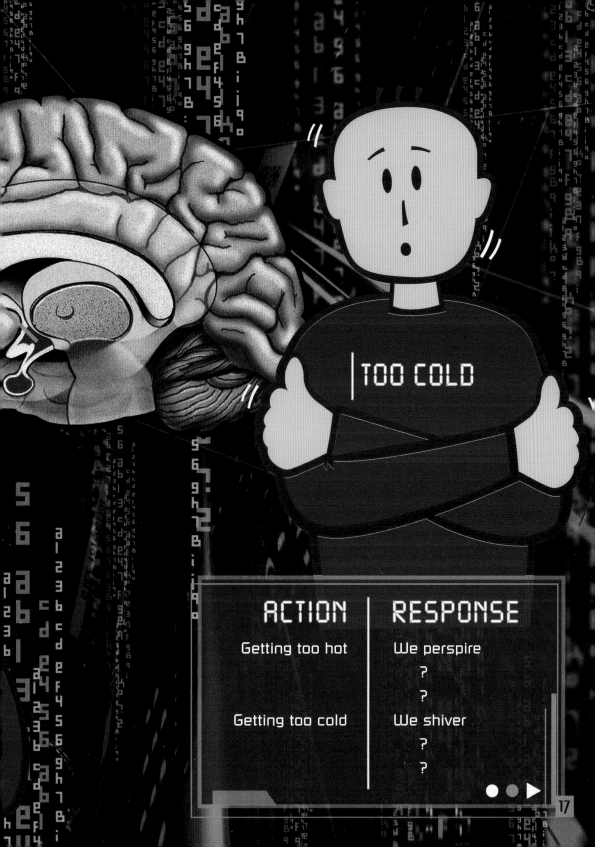

TOO COLD

ACTION	RESPONSE
Getting too hot	We perspire ? ?
Getting too cold	We shiver ? ?

ANIMAL BRAINS

Humans are more intelligent than any other animal. Their brains are the most complicated.

Every animal is born with instincts — things it can do automatically. Many animals survive on instincts alone. But others have the ability to learn skills by using their brain.

Even the simplest and tiniest animal brain can do amazing things.

The honeybee has a tiny brain and yet it can learn which flowers give the best pollen and at which times of the day.

Honeybees can also pass on information they have learned to other bees by doing a "waggle" dance.

QUESTION:

Honeybees can also pass on information they have learned to other bees by doing a "waggle" dance.

What questions might you ask about this information?

Monkeys and apes have similar brains as ours. They have to use their brains to help them solve problems. They can analyze situations before deciding what to do. Very few animals can manage this kind of thought.

The nutcracker bird stores pine seeds in up to a thousand different places and can find them all again.

▶ Problem solved: A tool is used to crack a nut.

▶ The nutcracker bird uses memory to find a hidden seed.

CLARIFY:
▶ ANALYZE

A fix

B figure out

C think about

A, B, OR C ?

21

HOW BRAINS & COMPUTERS COMPARE

Computers and brains are powered by different types of energy, but they both use electrical signals to send information.

Most computers send electric signals through wires, but our brains send signals through our nerve cells.

Computers and brains do have things that are similar.

Computers and brains both store memories.

Computers and brains can both perform new tasks. A computer can be given new hardware and software, and our brains can learn new things.

The inside of a computer is protected by a hard cover. Our brains are protected by our skulls. The top part of the skull surrounds the brain and forms a protective shield. This helps stop our brain from getting crushed.

ELECTRICAL SIGNALS TO SEND INFORMATION

QUESTION:

What do you think might happen if our nerve cells were damaged?

However, if a computer is dropped or infected by a virus, it can be repaired. It is not so easy to repair our brains. They are fragile and do not have replacement parts.

Although computers can do amazing things at great speeds, they cannot laugh, cry, love, dream, or think like our brains can. This is what makes us human beings.

Scientists are making computers that behave in more and more human ways. However, there is still so much that is unknown about how the human brain works that so far, no computer has yet been able to imitate it.

▶ This computerized dog can move but it cannot lick your hand or love you.

COMPARE & CONTRAST:

THE WAY A COMPUTER WORKS	THE WAY THE BRAIN WORKS
?	?
?	?

It is an exciting time in the study of the brain.

Different types of new technologies are being used to make important discoveries.

Scientists are always trying to find more about the secret life of our brains.

INDEX

animal brains 18, 20

comparing brains and
computers 22, 24

controlling body temperature . . . 16

cortex 4

hypothalamus 16

left side of brain 4

memory

      long-term 12

      short-term 14

neurons 6

receiving and interpreting
information 4, 6

REM sleep 10

right side of brain 4

sleeping brain 8, 10

▶ Studying brain scans reveals information about our brains.

KEY POINTS

The brain is the control
room that directs our
thinking ...

?

?

?

INTERESTING FACTS

It operates 24 hours
a day ...

?

?

?

FIND SOME MORE KEY POINTS AND INTERESTING FACTS

● ● ▶

THINK ABOUT THE TEXT

Making connections – What connections can you make to *Brain Matter*?

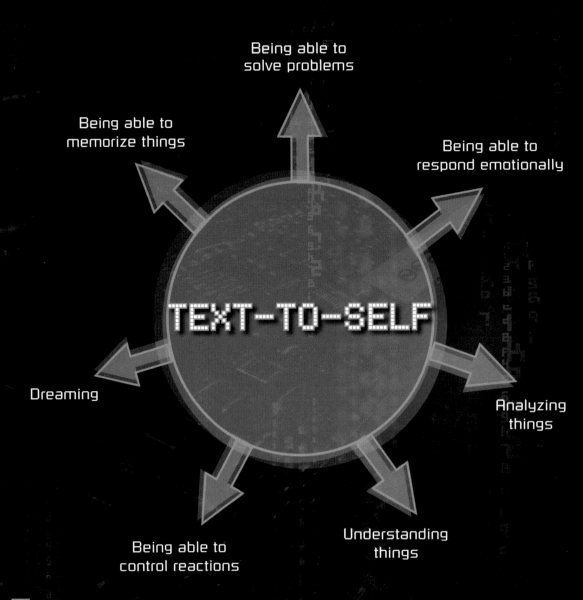

Being able to
solve problems

Being able to
memorize things

Being able to
respond emotionally

TEXT-TO-SELF

Dreaming

Analyzing
things

Being able to
control reactions

Understanding
things

TEXT-TO-TEXT

Talk about other informational texts you may have
read that have similar features. Compare the texts.

TEXT-TO-WORLD

Talk about situations in the world
that connect to elements in the text.

PLANNING AN INFORMATIONAL EXPLANATION

1 Select a topic that explains why something is the way it is or how something works.

2 Make a mind map of questions about the topic, e.g.:

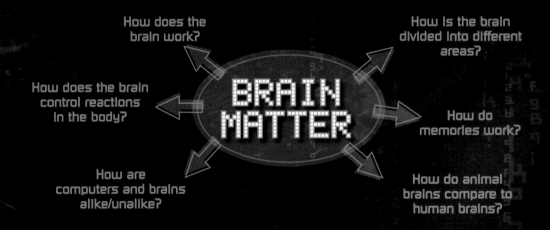

How does the brain work?

How is the brain divided into different areas?

How does the brain control reactions in the body?

BRAIN MATTER

How do memories work?

How are computers and brains alike/unalike?

How do animal brains compare to human brains?

3 Locate the information that you need.

library

Internet

experts

4 Organize your information using the questions you selected as headings.

5 Make a plan.

Introduction

Points in a coherent and logical sequence

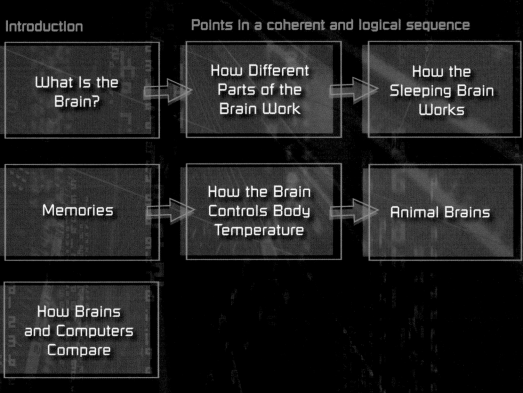

What Is the Brain?

How Different Parts of the Brain Work

How the Sleeping Brain Works

Memories

How the Brain Controls Body Temperature

Animal Brains

How Brains and Computers Compare

6 Design some visuals to include in your explanation. You can use graphs, diagrams, labels, charts, tables, cross-sections . . .

AN INFORMATIONAL EXPLANATION

A Explores causes and effects

B Uses scientific and technical vocabulary

C Uses the present tense

D Is written in a formal style that is concise and accurate

E Avoids author opinion